Dear Parent:
Your child's love of reading starts here!

Every child learns to read in a different way and at his or her own speed. Some go back and forth between reading levels and read favorite books again and again. Others read through each level in order. You can help your young reader improve and become more confident by encouraging his or her own interests and abilities. From books your child reads with you to the first books he or she reads alone, there are I Can Read Books for every stage of reading:

SHARED READING
Basic language, word repetition, and whimsical illustrations, ideal for sharing with your emergent reader

BEGINNING READING
Short sentences, familiar words, and simple concepts for children eager to read on their own

READING WITH HELP
Engaging stories, longer sentences, and language play for developing readers

READING ALONE
Complex plots, challenging vocabulary, and high-interest topics for the independent reader

ADVANCED READING
Short paragraphs, chapters, and exciting themes for the perfect bridge to chapter books

I Can Read Books have introduced children to the joy of reading since 1957. Featuring award-winning authors and illustrators and a fabulous cast of beloved characters, I Can Read Books set the standard for beginning readers.

A lifetime of discovery begins with the magical words **"I Can Read!"**

Visit www.icanread.com for information
on enriching your child's reading experience.

Huff and Puff Copyright © 2012 by HarperCollins Publishers. All rights reserved. Manufactured in China. No part of this book may be used or reproduced in any manner whatsoever without written permission except in the case of brief quotations embodied in critical articles and reviews. For information address HarperCollins Children's Books, a division of HarperCollins Publishers, 10 East 53rd Street, New York, NY 10022.
www.icanread.com

Library of Congress catalog card number: 2013942757
ISBN 978-0-06-230502-2 (trade bdg.) — ISBN 978-0-06-230501-5 (pbk. bdg.)

13 14 15 16 17   SCP   10 9 8 7 6 5 4 3 2 1
❖
First Edition

I Can Read! My First SHARED READING

Huff and Puff

by Tish Rabe
pictures by Gill Guile

HARPER
An Imprint of HarperCollinsPublishers

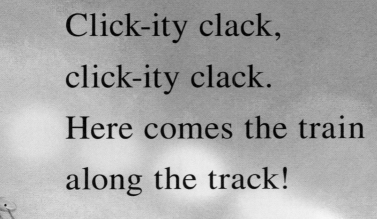

Click-ity clack,
click-ity clack.
Here comes the train
along the track!

Huff in front.

Puff in back.

Click-ity, click-ity clack.

Puff helps Huff.
Puff pushes the train
in winter snow
and summer rain.

Click-ity, click-ity clack.

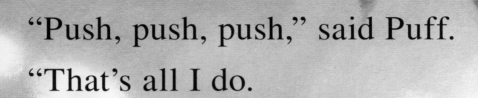

"Push, push, push," said Puff. "That's all I do.

I think it's time
for something new."

"I want to pull the train,"
said Puff.

"That's just fine with me,"
said Huff.

So the train went
down the track.
Puff in front.

Huff in back.

Click-ity, click-ity clack.

15

But then the wind
began to blow.

Puff said, "Oh, no!
Here comes the snow!"

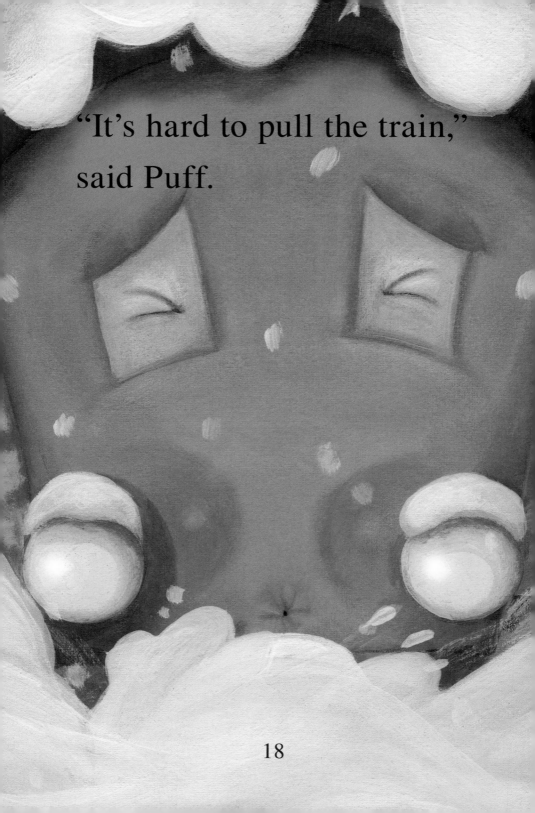

"It's hard to pull the train,"
said Puff.

"It's hard to push the train,"
said Huff.

"I tried," said Puff,
"but now I see:
In back is the place for me."

"I tried," said Huff,
"but now I see:
In front is the place for me."

21

So now the train goes
down the track
Huff in front.

Puff in back.

23

Click-ity, click-ity clack.